A STRANGER'S CHILDREN

MAIL ORDER BRIDES OF MINE'S PLACE

SUSANNAH CALLOWAY

Tica House
Publishing

Sweet Romance that Delights and Enchants!

PERSONAL WORD FROM THE AUTHOR

Dearest Readers,

Thank you so much for choosing one of my books. I am proud to be a part of the team of writers at Tica House Publishing who work joyfully to bring you stories of hope, faith, courage, and love. Your kind words and loving readership are deeply appreciated.

I would like to personally invite you to sign up for updates and to become part of our **Exclusive Reader Club**—it's completely Free to join! We'd love to welcome you!

Much love,

Susannah Calloway

VISIT HERE to Join our Reader's Club and to Receive Tica House Updates!

https://wesrom.subscribemenow.com/

CONTENTS

CHAPTER 1

The general store smelled like fresh pine and brown sugar. Mike Keating had always loved the smell, ever since his first memories of scampering across the empty, grassy space where his father, Joseph, sawed the pine planks that now creaked under Mike's feet as he trudged across the store. He'd grown up in this store, helping his father to weigh out the goods, pretending to talk tough with the men who came in for mining supplies or salt pork or rope or nails, eventually hiding behind the counter when the girls his age would bat their eyelashes at him.

All the girls except Clara, of course. Mike had never hidden from her.

No, he told himself. *Don't think about Clara. It doesn't do any good.* He pushed the thought of her out of his mind and set down the wooden box at his feet. Moving quickly, his muscular shoulders chafing against his plain blue button-up shirt, Mike lifted cans of baked beans from the box and onto one of the empty shelves.

As he worked, a thin wind howled around the corners of the general store, its piercing voice singing songs of the coming winter. Mike worked all the faster at the sound of it, burying his thoughts in the order forms he wanted to fill out this evening before he went home. He'd need to order plenty of extra stock if he wanted the people of Mine's Place, Colorado Territory, to have everything they needed when the long winter set in. Sometimes the trains just couldn't get through after November or so.

November. The thought of that month made Mike's stomach tie itself in knots. It was November first that he lost Clara.

Clara. He pushed the thought away again, but it was so difficult not to remember her. Her laugh had been as silvery as starlight in bare branches. Some days he thought he still heard it echoing through the house they'd shared with his parents.

Some days it was the reason why he stayed in the store late, restocking or sweeping or filling out order forms, rather than face the absence of that sweet voice in his parents' home.

Still, he couldn't avoid his home forever.

By the time Mike locked up the store and stepped onto the boardwalk, no one else was out and about anymore. All the houses of the tiny town were snugly locked up against the bitter wind that howled through the night, and wisps of smoke rose from their chimneys, warm firelight leaping in the windows. Even the saloon just down the street was closed and shuttered, although Mike could still hear a few bursts of brawny laughter from within.

The wind nipped at his nose and ears. The first snow wouldn't be long now, he thought.

His boots clumped on the boardwalk as he followed it up the street to the cozy home at the far end. Joseph's home had been one of the first wooden houses here, back when the rest of this town had lived in miner's tents at the peak of the Pike's Peak Gold Rush. Mike remembered well when this home had been nothing but a cottage. He himself had painted every single plank of the addition on the south side; a whole suite he'd once shared with Clara...

Why couldn't he stop thinking of Clara tonight? Mike rubbed a hand over his face to ease his headache and pushed open the front door.

"Ma, it's me," he yelled.

He walked into the kitchen to find it warm and fragrant with the scent of Kathleen Keating's fantastic rabbit pie. His mother looked up from the stove: a plump, comfortable figure in her checkered dress and long white apron.

6

"I was starting to worry about you, honey," she said. "Where were you?"

"Sorry, Ma. Just had to finish up some order forms." Mike hugged her from behind and planted a kiss on the back of her neck. "Smells good."

"Rabbit pie, just like your sister loves." Kathleen's face lit up. "They'll be here any minute now. Hurry and wash up so that we can eat."

"You're the boss," Mike teased.

Kathleen swatted at him with a dishcloth. "Hurry." she ordered.

Mike returned from a brief wash to find that Joseph was already sitting at the table, sipping a cup of strong black coffee. The weathered lines of Joseph's face made him look far older than his years, half hidden by a mad bush of white beard and mustache.

"How are things in the store, son?" Joseph asked.

"All good, Pa. I'm just making sure we'll have enough supplies for the winter," said Mike.

Joseph's mustache spread out as he smiled. "That's my boy." He patted Mike's arm. "I know it's only been three months since I let you take over the running of the store, but you know exactly what you're doing. I'm proud of you, my boy."

"Thanks, Pa." Mike's smile returned easily at those words, and his leaden heart lifted slightly.

It lifted further still when there was a knock at the door, and Pa's old hound dog raised his head from his blanket by the stove and let out one single wheezy bark. Mike went to open the door and grinned at the sight of his sister and her husband. Emma had her mother's plump red cheeks, and they seemed to be glowing brighter than ever tonight as she smiled up at him from behind the casserole dish wrapped in cloths that she carried in her hands.

"Emmy, it's good to see you." Mike embraced his sister gently.

"Careful, it's hot." Emma laughed.

"Come on inside." Mike pulled the door open and gripped his brother-in-law's hand warmly. "Caleb, how are you?"

"Good, thank you, Mike. Very good." Caleb grinned.

They all went through into the kitchen, where Emma put down the dish and exchanged hugs with everyone, Joseph staying seated on account of his bad back. Caleb almost bowed in deference when he shook Joseph's hand.

Emma and Kathleen started dishing up dinner. Mike and Caleb sat down facing one another as the women chatted happily. Caleb was a burly man, with his shirt collar unbuttoned, his neck and face permanently blasted by sunburn even at this time of the year, marking him for the cattle rancher he was.

"How's the store doing, Mike?" Caleb asked.

"It's good," said Mike. "Stocking up for winter, you know."

"Good. Good to hear." Caleb cleared his throat and rubbed the back of his neck.

"Let's take hands," said Joseph gruffly.

They joined hands around the table, and Joseph led them in a simple table grace before they started tucking into the delicious, hearty dinner.

"Wonderful as always, Ma," said Mike.

"Excuse me, what about the vegetables I brought?" Emma pressed a hand to her heart in mock indignation.

"Eh, they'll do," said Mike.

"Michael." Kathleen chided. "Don't tease your sister like that."

Emma laughed. "Don't worry, Ma. He's been doing it all our lives. I doubt he'll ever stop."

Kathleen chuckled. "Quite right. So do I."

Emma and Caleb exchanged a glance. There was a brief silence, and Mike noticed how Caleb lightly squeezed his wife's hand before turning back to his meal. Emma's eyes met Mike's.

"Well, Mike, soon you'll have the chance to really enjoy your childishness," she said.

Mike raised an eyebrow. "What do you mean?"

"I mean that you're going to be an uncle," said Emma.

Mike blinked at her. "What?"

Kathleen's hands flew to her mouth, and she couldn't make a single sound.

Joseph frowned up at them. "What was that? I wasn't listening."

Emma laughed. "You lot aren't much good." She grinned. "Let me put it in plain words for you." She took a deep breath. "I'm going to have a baby."

"*We're* going to have a baby." Caleb grinned from ear to ear.

"Emma, my sweet child." Kathleen flew to her feet and flung her arms around Emma's neck. "I'm going to be a grandmother. Oh, I don't believe it. Congratulations."

Joseph beamed. "This is great news, Emma. Congratulations, Caleb."

Mike's heart felt as though it had turned to stone in his chest. He stared down at his half-empty plate, his appetite suddenly gone. It was only when Joseph gently nudged him under the table that he was able to raise his head and smile at his sister.

"I'm so happy for you, Emma." He reached over and squeezed her hands. "You're going to be a great mother."

Emma's eyes filled with happy tears. "Thank you, Mike." She laughed. "And you're going to be a great uncle."

Kathleen sagged back into her chair, her cheeks streaked with tears of joy. "Can you believe it, Joseph? We're going to be grandparents at last. Oh, Emma, when is the little one coming?"

"I saw Dr. Holmes today, and he said the baby's only coming in the early summer," said Emma. "So there's still plenty of time to build a crib."

"There's more than just a crib to build," said Joseph, laughing heartily.

Caleb blushed. "There's a lot to think about," he admitted. "But I'm excited." He wrapped an arm around Emma's shoulders. "*We're* excited to start our family."

Joseph raised his coffee mug. "A toast." he said. "To the growing Brown family."

"To the Browns." laughed Kathleen, her eyes shining.

Mike grabbed his mug and joined in, smiling as well as he could. It was only his mother who looked into his eyes and saw the suffering he was trying to hide.

~

Emma and Caleb had long gone, but Mike was still in the kitchen. He stood with his hands braced against the table, leaning on it as he stared out of the window. It was a perfect night now that the wind had died down, moonlit and silvery on the stern lines of Colorado's dry mountainsides.

Soft footsteps padded on the wooden floor behind him. "Still up?" said Kathleen softly.

Mike sighed, his shoulders sagging. "I'm all right, Ma. Go to bed."

"I know you're not, honey." Kathleen came up to him and rested a small, warm hand on his back. "I saw your eyes. You were trying to hide it for your sister's sake, but you can't hide a thing from your mother. You know that."

"I guess I do." Mike rubbed his face.

"What's wrong?" Kathleen asked. "You know you can tell me. Don't keep it bottled up, Michael. Not... the way you used to."

She carefully stepped around mentioning that first year after Clara died, the year when Mike had spent most of his time in the saloon, staring into the bottom of a glass. Knowing that that was the place he might go again if he didn't share his feelings spurred Mike to talk about them now.

"It's selfish," he said.

"No, it isn't. Selfish would be if you ruined your sister's happy evening. Instead, I saw you working hard to hide your sorrow," said Kathleen. "Come on, Michael. Tell me what it is."

Mike let out a long breath. His hands clenched into fists on the table.

"The day before she got sick..." He squeezed his eyes tight shut, as though that could hold back the pain of the memory. "You know how Clara and I were ready to start our family?"

Kathleen rubbed his back. "Yes, I do."

"Well, the day before she got so sick, she told me that she wanted a big family." Mike laughed softly. "At least six children."

"That sounds like Clara," said Kathleen.

"She would have been a perfect mother, Ma. You know that." Mike blinked back the tears that burned in his eyes. "It's been three years. Maybe we would have had one or two babies by now."

"I'm so sorry, honey," said Kathleen.

"I still don't know why she had to die." Mike choked the words out. "I miss her, Ma."

"We all do. Your wife was an angel, Michael," said Kathleen. "But you should know that you still have the chance to have something like that again."

Mike stared at her. "What are you talking about?"

Kathleen squeezed his arm. "You're still young, you know. Clara would want you to be happy. Don't you think it's time that you thought of remarrying?"

Mike let out a heavy sigh. Her words made his intestines knot, but he knew he had to face them. "I know she would," he mumbled. "But I don't know how to move on from her."

"You'll find your way, love." Kathleen hugged him. "You'll find your way."

Mike wasn't so sure.

CHAPTER 2

Selena Lintz grabbed her six-year-old son by the arm and yanked him back. "Look out." she cried.

The speeding carriage missed them both by inches. Its wheel smashed through a pile of ice-cold water, and it splattered on Selena's face and Wyatt's only clean shirt.

"Let me go, Mama." Wyatt snapped, ripping his tiny arm out of her grip.

On Selena's hip, Belle let out a long, squalling cry of protest.

"I'm sorry, baby. I'm sorry." Selena winced at the sight of muddy water all over her two-year-old daughter's face. She grasped the edge of her shawl and wiped it away. "It's all right. Don't cry, honey."

"Cold." Belle whimpered, clutching the front of Selena's dress with both chubby fists.

"I know, honey. We're almost going home," Selena promised. "Wyatt, get back here."

The little boy had already headed off to try crossing the street again. Selena grabbed his arm, ignoring his angry protests, and waited for a break in the madness of Boston traffic. The street was full, as always. Wagons and carriages rushed to and fro, while a mass of pedestrians, dogs, children, and livestock squeezed this way and that among them.

Finally spotting a break in the traffic, Selena dragged her children across the road and hurried along the sidewalk, keeping close to the soot-streaked buildings. This close to the docks, Boston's factories belched smoke into the air every hour of every day. Her nostrils were filled with the smell of salt, tar, and rotten fish.

"Don't touch that, Wyatt." she ordered.

The little boy reluctantly abandoned his quest to poke a dead rat lying in the nearby gutter. He jogged to keep up with Selena.

"Want go home," Belle whimpered.

"Almost, baby, almost," said Selena.

"I'm hungry," Wyatt whined.

"Mama's hungry too, love. We'll eat as soon as we get home," said Selena.

"What's for dinner?" Wyatt asked.

Selena's gut clenched at the thought. *Yesterday's bread and a few slices of hard cheese.* She couldn't say that to the boy. "We'll find out," she said.

They turned a corner, and the familiar sight of the old brick building by the docks greeted them. Selena felt her shoulders relax a little just looking at it. Even though she had been delighted to escape the orphanage and marry the man of her dreams, this was still the place where she'd felt safe enough as a child growing up. Safer by far than most of Boston's orphans, she supposed.

She walked up to the front door and knocked without hesitation. Wyatt sat down on the steps and started to poke a tiny bug with a piece of straw, which seemed like a relatively harmless activity. Selena rocked Belle on her hip, hoping to keep her from fussing just for a few minutes longer.

The door swung open, and a rush of relief ran through Selena. The sweet middle-aged woman standing in the door was Agnes, and she'd been the matron of Selena's dorm back when she was a child.

"Selena, honey." Agnes opened her arms. "How wonderful to see you. And the children, too."

Selena leaned gratefully into Agnes' hug, still holding Belle on her hip.

"They look well, dear," said Agnes, smiling at the children. Wyatt scowled up at her and went on poking the hapless bug.

"Wyatt, say hello," Selena ordered.

"Hello," Wyatt grunted.

Selena sighed. "I'm sorry, Agnes. He just hasn't been the same since—" She sucked in a breath.

"I know, dear," said Agnes softly. "It's only been a year. These things take time."

"I don't know if he'll ever go back to the happy little boy he was before John died." Selena wiped at her eyes.

"We can only trust the Lord to make that happen," said Agnes.

Selena hung her head. "I'm running low on trust."

Agnes studied her, worry in the lines around her eyes. "You're very pale, Selena. Has something happened?"

"Something… has been happening for a while," Selena admitted.

Agnes listened, wide-eyed.

"It's my parents-in-law." Selena bit her lip. "They were never happy about John marrying an orphan girl like me, as I'm sure you remember."

"Snobs, both of them," said Agnes.

"Maybe," said Selena. "Either way, they... they want me declared to be an unfit mother." Her eyes burned with tears. "Agnes, they want to take the children."

"They can't." said Agnes angrily.

"They can. Their lawyer is so—so nasty." Selena wiped at her tears. "I don't know how to stop this from happening, Agnes. I've done my best... I work every job I can. I take care of the children. But if they were taken away from me, I would have nothing." The thought made her chest feel closed and difficult to breathe with.

"Oh, Selena, I'm so sorry." Agnes took her free hand and squeezed it. "What can I do?"

"Pray," said Selena simply. "I don't have the words anymore, but I know you always do."

Agnes lowered her head immediately. "Father," she prayed softly, "You know every detail of what is happening in Selena's life. You know her strength, and You know her sorrow, and You know how badly she needs You. Please, Holy God, open a door for Selena. We don't know the way, but You do." She took a deep breath. "Amen."

"Amen," Selena whispered, but she could barely croak out the sound past the thick lump in her throat.

Belle wailed on Selena's hip. The child's thin voice rose through the chaos of the streets, cutting through the rattle of wheels and the clamor of voices. The pedestrian traffic was so thick that Selena almost had to shoulder her way through the crowd.

"Stay close, Wyatt," she ordered.

Wyatt sighed. "I'm right here, Mama."

"Hold my skirt," said Selena.

Wyatt scoffed. "I'm not a baby. I don't have to hold your skirt."

"Do it." Selena yelled.

Wyatt gave her a smoldering look and moodily grabbed onto her skirt. Selena's heart squeezed in her chest. She hated yelling, but it seemed that that was the only way for Wyatt to listen.

A scruffy-looking man brushed past them, much too close for comfort, and Selena's heart fluttered in her chest. She clutched Belle close and pawed frantically through the canvas bag she carried over her shoulder for a dry-mouthed few moments until her hand closed on her purse—a leather relic from a better time, a time before she lost John—and she felt that her handful of coins was still inside. Something loosened in her frightened chest, and she let out a breath. If they lost the only money she had left...

"Almost home, Wyatt," she said, quickening her pace.

There was no response from beside her, nor was there a tug at her skirt.

Selena looked down. The boy was gone.

"Wyatt?" she called, stopping in her tracks. She looked left and right, turned to look behind her. Up ahead, she saw nothing except a crush of strangers. "Wyatt." she yelled.

Her yell woke Belle, who had just begun to fall asleep on her shoulder. The toddler threw back her head and let out a long, wailing cry.

"It's all right, baby. It's all right," said Selena, but her voice was frantic, her hands shaking. She started forward, pushing through the crowd, almost running. "Wyatt." she screamed. "WYATT."

Then, blessedly, she spotted him. She shoved between a fat man and a gaggle of factory workers and saw him on the street corner, looking up at a quartet of younger ladies, who were cooing over him. The little boy was unharmed and sucking on a candy cane that one of them must have given him.

"Oh, he's just too precious for words." said one of the ladies. "Look at those curls."

"And those little red cheeks." sighed another.

"I hope one day I have a little boy just as adorable as he is," said the third.

"Oh, I'd like a girl first," said the fourth. She giggled. "But I guess we'll have to get our husbands first, won't we?"

"Soon." said the second. "Think about it, girls. In just a few weeks, one or more of us could be on a train out West to meet our husbands."

Giggling erupted among the girls just as Selena reached them. She grabbed Wyatt's arm, almost pulling his candy cane out of his mouth, and pulled him close. "How could you do this, Wyatt?" she cried. "You nearly killed me with fright."

The boy stared up at her. "I just went ahead, Mama."

"Oh, honey, you could have been lost." Selena cried. She pulled him close and looked up at the girls. "I'm sorry. This is my little boy. He—he just got away from me."

Belle was still crying. One of the ladies touched her shoulder. "Oh, hello, little one. Aren't you beautiful?"

Belle's wailing stopped instantly. She giggled, reaching her hands to the lady.

"Mama, they gave me candy." Wyatt waved the candy cane.

"Don't take candy from strangers," Selena chided. She blushed, turning to the young ladies. "I'm sorry, I didn't mean—"

"Of course not." The first girl tittered; she had black ringlets that spilled luxuriously over her shoulders. "I just couldn't resist. He's so sweet."

"Well, thank you. You probably stopped him from running into the street." Selena sighed. "Wyatt, you've been very naughty."

Wyatt glowered at her.

"Motherhood looks harder than I thought," said the second girl, a blonde, looking daunted.

"It's easier if your husband is alive." Selena managed a thin smile.

"Oh, you're a widow?" The black-haired girl's mouth turned down at the corners. "I'm sorry."

"You should ask the agency if they have a match for you." said the blonde.

Selena frowned. "The agency?"

"There," said the third girl, who had a mole on the corner of her lip. She pointed toward a small building directly behind her. "They're an agency to help girls like us find husbands."

"In the West." the blonde added with enthusiasm.

"The West?" Selena clutched Belle a little tighter. Two thoughts simultaneously fought for supremacy in her mind. The first was, *That's a long way from home.* The second was, *That's a long way from my parents-in-law and their lawyer.*

"Yes, that's right," said the blonde eagerly. "Since so many men went West in the gold rushes and that sort of thing, there's hardly any women out there, and they're starting to build towns and settle in."

"And so many of our young men died in the Civil War," the one with the mole added. "We've no suitors left. But there are plenty of men in the West."

"So you would go all that way to marry someone you've never met?" said Selena.

"Well, yes," said the black-haired one. "It's better than not being married at all. And besides, it's an adventure."

"We'll get to see a whole new part of the world," said the blonde, her eyes starry.

Selena looked at the agency and thought of Agnes' prayer, and she could practically hear the creak of a door swinging open before her. A terrifying door, to be sure—but one that would lead her far away from anyone who wanted to take her children away from her.

Would she marry a stranger to avoid being separated from her children? There was absolutely no question. Selena would do anything.

"Thank you," she said. "I—I think I'll do that." She tightened her grip on Wyatt's arm, turned to face the agency, and marched into it resolutely before she could change her mind.

CHAPTER 3

The agency was a blissful break from the cold outside. The room was small, but a cozy fire crackled in the little hearth, and Selena's wet shoes sank into a deep carpet as she stepped inside.

"Warm." Belle cooed and lowered her head onto Selena's shoulders.

Wyatt pulled away from her again, but it was only to scamper over to the fire and hold out his hands to warm them. Selena pushed down a familiar pang of guilt, ignoring that little inner voice that always told her, *Your parents-in-law are right. You are an incompetent mother.*

I'm a mother who will do anything for her children. Anything, Selena told herself. *Even this.*

She steeled herself with a deep breath and walked up to the counter on the far side of the room, where two women were sitting. One was absorbed in writing something; the other smiled up at her. She was young and pretty, with a gold wedding ring on her finger.

"Good evening. How can I help you?" she asked.

"I wanted to find out more about…" Selena thought of John and had to blink away tears. "About marrying someone in the West."

The woman glanced over her, reading the story that was written in her patched clothing and the unwashed face of the child on her hip. She gave a wide smile. "Moving West and becoming a mail-order bride can be a great way to start a whole new life."

"A whole new life," Selena echoed. She held Belle closer. "That sounds pretty good right now."

"I'll bet it does. See, we put you in touch with a man in the West looking for a wife. He pays for your ticket to his town, and when you get there, you marry him." The woman spread her hands. "It's simple. You can choose to correspond by mail for a while if you like, but it depends on the man and woman. And if you don't like him, well, then all you need to do is buy a ticket home."

Buy a ticket home. Selena didn't know how much that would cost, but she struggled to buy bread as it was. "That won't be an option for me," she admitted.

Again, the woman gave Belle a sympathetic glance. "Still, sometimes it's worth the risk. You could start over in the West. Forget about your hardships here... and escape anything that might be trying to harm you here in Boston."

Selena's shoulders sagged with the weight of the hardships that she'd endured in the past year, since John's death. She thought of her parents-in-law. Surely, they wouldn't pursue these children all the way to the West? Selena knew that their desire to take Belle and Wyatt away from her stemmed more from their contempt for her than from their love of the children. The children had barely met their grandparents at all in their short lives.

"I don't think I have any other choices," Selena said softly. "But tell me... do any of these men want women like me?" She choked the word out. "Widows."

"There are plenty of those these days, since the war," said the woman. "Widows with children—well, those are a little harder."

Selena held Belle closer. "I won't leave them behind."

"Of course not." The woman smiled. "Sometimes we find men who don't mind—or are even looking for—a wife with children from a previous marriage." She turned to the woman writing the letter. "Don't we, Glenda?"

Glenda looked up. "What?"

"Have suitors looking for women with children," said the younger woman.

Glenda scoffed. "Not all that often." She looked up at Selena. "Are you looking for a husband?"

"Yes," said Selena, before she could stop herself.

"Then you're in luck. We have one right now," said Glenda. "Show her Charles Ellsworth, Tiffany."

"Of course." said Tiffany. "He only wrote to us yesterday, but he'll be perfect." She pulled out a letter and showed it to Selena. "Charles Ellsworth is a childless widower himself. He's older, but he has a successful ranch, and he longs for children. He specified that he didn't mind marrying a widow with children."

Selena Ellsworth. She pushed away the thought. "Where does he live?"

"Let me see." Tiffany checked the letter. "Oh, here it is. Mine's Place, Colorado Territory."

Selena had never even heard of Mine's Place, but she knew Colorado Territory was a long, long way away. A tremor ran through her at the thought of making that journey with two small children. Belle had never even been on a train before.

"He's an educated man," Tiffany added. "And he seems very kind." She held out the letter. "He could give you and your children a good life."

Selena tried to read the neat copperplate writing, but her mind was racing. Could she look into the eyes of another man and say, "I do", so soon after losing John? He'd been sunshine in her life. He'd made the world better. He'd given her the greatest gifts of all: Belle and Wyatt.

And it was her responsibility to raise them the way John would have wanted.

Yours sincerely,

Charles Ellsworth.

The end of the letter jolted her out of her memories, and she thought again of being Mrs. Ellsworth instead of Mrs. Brown. She wouldn't belong to John anymore.

"I don't know." Selena's voice trembled as she handed the letter back. "I… I don't know if I'm ready to remarry."

"You don't have much choice, by the looks of it," grunted Glenda.

"Glenda." Tiffany chided.

"I'm just speaking the truth." Glenda laid down her pen and looked up at Selena. "Despite what my optimistic colleague thinks, we hardly ever have men who would accept a woman with children. Your chances of finding another match are next to nothing. Take this chance while you can."

Tiffany grimaced. "I'm sorry for Glenda's harshness, but she's not wrong. We really do have men like this only on the odd occasion."

Wyatt's small hand tugged at Selena's skirt. She looked down into his wide brown eyes, so very much like his father's, and felt everything inside her soften.

"Mama, can we stay here?" he asked. "It's so much warmer than home."

Selena's heart felt torn in half. She reached down and ruffled her son's hair. "Oh, honey..." She swallowed hard, and looked at the letter again. "Soon we'll have a new home. And it'll always be warm there."

Wyatt's eyes lit up. "Really?"

"Yes, baby. Really." Selena turned to Tiffany, her body cold with determination. "Write to Charles Ellsworth. I'd like to be his—" She swallowed. "His bride."

Mike ignored the ache in his feet as he poured another small measure of flour onto the scales. The two-pound weight rose, and he added just a little more, until the weight was slightly higher than the pan containing the flour.

"Oh, Mr. Keating, that's too much," the old lady on the other side of the counter protested. "I only wanted two pounds."

"Oh no, ma'am. It looks very much like two pounds exactly to me." Mike poured the flour into a sack.

The old woman's cheeks flushed faintly. She still held herself with pride, but her dress had grown more and more patched and faded since her husband had died in a mining accident on Pike's Peak last winter.

"Thank you," she murmured softly.

"Anytime, ma'am." Mike pushed the sack across the counter toward her and accepted her payment. While she was busy buttoning up her purse, he slipped a couple of apples into the sack while she wasn't looking.

She bustled away, and Mike turned to look for the next customer, but the store was empty for the first time all day. He let out a little sigh of relief and turned to the storeroom. It was time for a cup of coffee. He hadn't had anything since breakfast, and it was well past noon.

As he poured thick black coffee into an enamel mug, the bell over the shop door rang. He set the mug aside and hurried up to the counter with his best smile, but this time, it wasn't a customer; instead, an older lady strode inside, followed by a girl about Mike's age.

"Ah, good morning, Mrs. Spencer." Mike grinned. "Do you have the produce I ordered?"

"All the best of the last harvest, young man," said Mrs. Spencer. "Pumpkins, beets, apples, potatoes—plenty of things to can and preserve."

"Wonderful. Thank you so much. I'm glad to be able to stock my storeroom before the winter," said Mike. He looked up at the younger woman, who had black hair and deep, dark eyes. "Hello, Rachel."

She batted long, dark lashes. "Hello, Mike."

Mike turned back to Mrs. Spencer. "It's such a long drive. Would you like some coffee?"

"Yes, that would be good, thank you," said Mrs. Spencer.

Mike offered her a seat behind the counter and his untouched coffee. "I'll unload the wagon and be right back," he told her.

"I'll help," said Rachel quickly.

She followed him outside. For once, balmy sunshine trickled out of the pale blue sky, and a few kids played in the street. As always, Mike tried not to stare at them. Clara used to love watching the kids play…

You'll find your way. He reminded himself of his mom's words about moving on from Clara and clung to them.

The wagon waited around the back of the store, a contented mule munching from a nosebag in the harness. Mike patted the mule and opened the back of the wagon.

"Here," said Rachel. "I'll hand things to you, and you can carry them to the storeroom."

"Just be careful with the heavy bags," Mike cautioned her.

Rachel laughed merrily. "I'm the oldest daughter of a farmer. I practically grew up doing the work of three boys."

Mike grinned back at her. She had a nice laugh, he realized. Carefree and unpretentious.

She grabbed a bag of squash and hauled it across the floor to him. Mike took it, his fingers digging into the sackcloth, and hoisted it onto his shoulder. He added another before plodding into the storeroom and dumping the bags down on the floor.

They worked in silence for several minutes. When they started unloading the massive orange pumpkins near the front of the wagon, Rachel finally spoke up.

"Have you heard about the winter dance?" she asked.

Mike scooped a pumpkin into his arms and held them out for another. "Ma mentioned something about it. It's in December, isn't it?"

"Mid-December," Rachel confirmed. "Six weeks away. They say it's going to be fun. The saloon band will play, and my mama, too, on the celeste."

"She plays well," Mike grunted. He plodded into the storeroom with the two pumpkins.

When he got back to the wagon, Rachel went on. "I think everyone will be there. We can all do with some cheering up at the beginning of winter, don't you think?"

"I do." said Mike. He took another pumpkin from her.

"I hear some of the men are asking women to the dance." Rachel's words came out in a rush, and there was a blush on her cheeks as she said them. Her eyes darted to his, then away.

Mike almost dropped the pumpkin in his arms. He turned and stumbled to the storeroom, his heart thudding. It was obvious to him that she wanted him to ask her to the dance.

The thought of dancing with another woman was strange, but at the same time, he thought of the happy glow in Emma's face. When last had he been so happy? When last had he felt that his life was moving forward?

You'll find your way. Maybe this was the way.

Mike screwed up all his courage as he strode back out to the wagon. They'd unloaded everything, and Rachel hopped down, then expertly closed the wooden tailgate.

"Well, that's it, then." She slapped her hands clean and smiled up at Mike. "Thanks for your help. It's nice working with someone so... strong." Her eyes wandered to his shoulders.

Her interest gave him the courage to say the words, but they still came out fast and jumbled: "Doyouwanttogotothewinterdancewithme?"

Rachel blinked. "What?"

"I mean—would you like to go to the winter dance with me?" Mike managed.

Rachel blushed prettily and ran a hand through her black hair. "Mike, I—I would love to do that." She giggled.

"Good." Mike managed a smile of his own. "That'll be nice."

They walked back into the store in silence, but Rachel was beaming.

CHAPTER 4

"Mine's Place," the conductor called.

Selena raised her exhausted head from where she had
pillowed it on the windowsill. Somehow, she'd finally gotten
Wyatt and Belle to sleep. After yet another long night—their
fifth on the train—of whining, complaining about the sound,
waking other passengers, and crying, the children had finally
dozed off just a few minutes ago.

At least, it felt like they'd been asleep just a few minutes.
When Selena checked her cracked brass pocket watch, she
realized that it was late afternoon already.

She peered out of the window. Golden light fell across a
landscape so harsh that she couldn't help sucking in a breath
of shock. Mountains rose against the horizon, sharp and
jagged, like the teeth of a mad dog. Clumps of brush and pine

trees clung to a landscape that seemed to be composed mainly of rocks and shale. There were no green fields and lush woods here, nothing like the countryside surrounding Boston.

It took her a moment to pick out the town of Mine's Place on the flanks of one of the mountainsides, and the sight of it made her heart plummet into her belly. This little place was hardly any bigger than a single city block in Boston. Wisps of woodsmoke rose from the chimneys; only one of the roads was paved, and the train tracks stopped dead here. This must be the furthest reach of this branch of railroad.

"Mine's Place." the conductor yelled again.

Selena nudged Wyatt's shoulder. "Wyatt, baby, we're here."

He sat up, his hair sticking up in an endearing cowlick. "We're in the Wild West?" he cried, his eyes sparkling.

"Yes. Stay close to me now. Bring your case," Selena ordered.

Wyatt gave her a moody glare and tugged the tiny suitcase—containing almost everything they owned—out from under the seat. Trying not to wake Belle, Selena cradled the child in the crook of one arm and pulled her canvas bag over her shoulder with her free hand. Apart from a man with a sack of mail, they were the only passengers left on the train, and they disembarked onto a tiny wooden platform at the end of the paved road. The man with the mail followed, tossed the sack into the arms of a waiting lackey, and then disappeared back into the train.

Selena tried not to tremble as she clutched Belle and looked around. She had no idea what Charles Ellsworth looked like, but she had half expected to see him standing on the platform with an expectant look. Maybe even a bunch of flowers, in some of her dreams…

But there was no one on the station at all. No one except the man with the bag of mail. He wandered over to the post office, directly across the paved street, and disappeared inside.

"Where's the man who's going to take us to our new home, Mama?" Wyatt asked.

"He must be on his way, dear," said Selena. "Come… let's sit over here."

Her limbs trembling with exhaustion, Selena led the children over to the single bench at the edge of the platform. Belle stirred slightly as she sat down, and she rocked the toddler, hushing her back to sleep. Wyatt set the case down and looked around, wide-eyed and fascinated.

"Why are there so few houses?" he asked.

"Because this is the frontier, honey," said Selena. "Not a city."

"Wow." Wyatt's eyes were huge. "It's the *Wild* West."

Hooves clopped on the road, and Selena looked up, heart pounding. A cowboy rode down the street on a stocky little horse, silver detailing flashing on his saddle. She rose to her feet, but he jogged on by the platform without sparing her a second glance.

"Look, Mama." Wyatt let go of her skirt and ran forward. "A cowboy."

"Wyatt, get back here." Selena gasped. The man on horseback had a large revolver on each hip.

"But look at his *guns*, Mama. And his hat." Wyatt pointed at the white Stetson the man wore.

"I said, *get back here*." Selena yelled.

Wyatt moped back over to her, gave her a morose glare, and flung himself down on the bench beside her.

"Now sit right here, and don't you dare get off this bench, do you understand?" Selena snapped.

Wyatt gave her another glare but said nothing.

They sat in silence. Belle slept on; Wyatt's arms were folded, and he kept kicking his heels against the simple wooden bench, which grew more and more uncomfortable as time ticked by. The shadows lengthened, and a chill crept across the mountains, colder and sharper than Boston's insidious winter damp. Selena cuddled Belle closer and kept a sharp eye on Wyatt. He was wearing his only coat, and his fingers were already growing pale with cold.

A few wagons went by, but none stopped. In fact, no one gave Selena or the children so much as a glance.

"I'm bored, Mama," Wyatt complained. He jumped up off the bench.

"Sit back down," Selena ordered.

"Why?" Wyatt demanded. "I just want to walk around the platform."

"Please, honey. Just sit down. I don't want you to get knocked over," said Selena. *Or shot, or stolen, or bitten by a snake—aren't there poisonous snakes here?*

Wyatt let out an exaggerated sigh and sat again with a thump.

The thump woke Belle, who squirmed in Selena's arms. The toddler's eyes snapped open, and she let out a whimper.

"It's all right, Belle. You're all right." Selena rocked her. "Shhhh, there. You're all right."

Belle was unconvinced. Her whimper became a cry.

Wyatt jumped up from the bench again.

"Get back here, Wyatt." Selena snapped.

Her voice only made Belle cry louder. The little girl clutched at Selena's dress, squirming and kicking in her arms, and Wyatt ran across the platform to gape at an ox wagon as it rumbled past without slowing down.

"Wyatt." Selena snapped. She hugged Belle closer. "Shhh, shhh. All right, baby girl. Shhh."

Belle only cried all the louder.

Tears stung the corners of Selena's eyes as she rocked the toddler as well as she could. Where were they going to go? She had only a few pennies in her pocket. It wouldn't keep them alive for long. Where would they sleep? Where was Charles Ellsworth?

Had she brought them all the way out here to die? The thought sent an appalling chill through her veins.

"Wyatt, please." Selena cried, tears filling her eyes.

Belle's cheeks were wet and scarlet with tears, and Selena kissed her forehead, trying to soothe her, but her crying only grew louder.

"Are you all right, dear?"

The calm, soft voice cut through the chaos like sunbeams through a storm. Selena looked up into a plump, rosy-cheeked face, framed by gray hair. Friendly, warm eyes twinkled down at her.

"I—I'm—" Selena stopped. She couldn't tell this stranger how afraid she was, but saying *I'm all right* was a lie so blatant that it would not pass her lips.

"I'm Kathleen Keating." The older woman reached out and brushed the back of her hand over Belle's cheek. "Hello, little one."

Belle's sobs grew abruptly silent. She stared up at Kathleen, tears still rolling down her cheeks.

"Thank you." Selena let out a breath. "It's been a long road for us."

Kathleen gave her clothes a curious look. "Where are you from?"

"Boston," said Selena.

Kathleen let out a low whistle. "That's a long, long way, all right." Her accent drawled softly.

Wyatt appeared at Selena's hip. "You sound funny," he said.

"Wyatt." Selena scolded.

Kathleen laughed merrily. "I think *you* sound funny, young man."

"I don't." Wyatt protested, giggling.

Kathleen's eyes met Selena's. "What's brought you all the way out here, then?"

Selena's heart trembled within her. She couldn't help pouring out the truth to those kind eyes. "I'm here to marry a man. I'm—I'm a mail order bride."

Kathleen's eyes widened fractionally. "I've heard of that." She paused. "Now who are you marrying, dear? It's not right to leave a lady with children waiting like this."

Selena swallowed. "Charles Ellsworth," she said. "Do you know him?"

Instantly, Kathleen's face fell. She stepped back, horror in her eyes as she looked at the children.

"What is it?" Selena cried. "Why are you looking at them like that? Is he—does he—is he a drunkard? A womanizer?" The tears threatened to escape her eyes now.

"Oh, no, honey, none of those things. Charles was a lovely, lovely man," said Kathleen. "He would have been a perfect husband for you, but—"

"*Was?*" Selena croaked.

Kathleen rested a hand on her arm. "I'm so sorry, dear. Charles is dead. He was killed by a snakebite just last week."

Selena's knees gave out under her. She fell onto the bench with a thump, prompting Belle to start crying again. She couldn't find it within her to rock the baby or even murmur reassurances. Instead, Selena simply stared up at Kathleen, aware that her entire world was falling apart around her. Her stomach felt twisted into knots.

"My children," she croaked out. "My babies. Where will I go with my babies?" Hot tears spilled down her cheeks, and she made no move to stop them.

"Do you know anyone in Mine's Place?" Kathleen asked.

"No." Selena sobbed the words out. "I only know people in Boston, and those are my parents-in-law, and they want to take the children away from me. My poor John has been dead only a year, and I'm going to lose the children, and—"

"No," said Kathleen firmly.

Selena stared up at her.

"You're not going to lose the children." Kathleen's voice was very calm. She bent and picked up the suitcase that Wyatt had shoved under the bench.

"Wh-what are you doing?" Selena stammered out.

"You're coming home with me," said Kathleen firmly. "We have enough to share with those in need and an extra room in the house, so you may as well come. There are plenty of opportunities in Mine's Place for a pretty, intelligent girl like you. You'll find one, I'm sure. And for tonight, you can stay with us."

Selena was shocked clean out of her tears. She sat staring up at Kathleen. "Why would you do such a thing?"

"Oh, honey, don't you know?" said Kathleen. "Our Lord told us that whoever gives food or shelter or comfort to the least of these gives it to Him." She laughed softly. "Now come on, Selena. Let's get you out of this cold wind before it gets dark."

Kathleen grasped her arm gently, and with her crying toddler on her hip and Wyatt scampering along behind, Selena found herself blindly following this kind woman down the main road of this strange place.

Mike pulled the storeroom window shut and latched it firmly, then gave it a little rattle to make sure it was secure. Mine's Place had become much safer in the past couple of years, but this was still the Wild West, after all.

Satisfied that the window was safely shut, Mike locked the door behind him and stepped into the general store. He was surprised to hear the bell over the front door jingling; it was already just past closing time, and he'd already flipped the sign on the door to CLOSED.

Oh, well. It must be one last desperate customer. No harm in helping them. Mike forced a smile back onto his tired face.

The woman who stepped into the store certainly looked desperate. Her cheeks were smudged with dirt, and her striking, jade-green eyes were reddened with tears. She held a toddler on her hip, and a silent, morose little boy followed her inside, hanging onto her skirt.

Mike was about to greet her when Kathleen followed the little family into the store.

"There." said Kathleen. "Much warmer in here. This is my son, Michael."

"Hello." Mike raised an eyebrow to his mother, then smiled at the woman. "I go by Mike."

"Selena," said the woman.

"I'm Wyatt," announced the little boy. He marched up to the counter and held out a hand.

"*Wyatt*." Selena sounded exhausted.

"Hello, Wyatt." Mike reached over the counter and shook the tiny hand. "It's nice to meet you."

Wyatt flashed a huge, heart-melting grin.

"Why don't you choose a piece of candy, Wyatt?" Kathleen asked.

"Do you mean it?" Wyatt gasped, as though he hadn't seen candy in months.

"I do," said Kathleen. "Go on."

He scampered off, and Selena trailed after him, looking lost.

"I haven't seen them around town before," Mike commented in a low voice.

"That's because they haven't been here for long." Kathleen sighed and leaned on the counter. "Remember how Charles Ellsworth told us that he was getting a mail-order bride?"

"Poor Charles, God rest his soul. He was so excited," said Mike, sighing.

Kathleen gave him a long look.

Mike straightened up. "No. Surely—"

"I'm afraid so," said Kathleen. "This poor girl was coming here to be Charles' wife. But since they never married, of course, she has no right to any of the inheritance. She's got nothing, Michael."

Mike watched as, across the store, the adorable little boy struggled to choose between a gumball and a candy cane.

"Her husband died a year ago," Kathleen went on in a hushed voice. "Leaving her with the two little ones."

"That's terrible," said Mike softly.

Kathleen nodded. "She has nowhere to go, no one to turn to. Her parents are dead and her parents-in-law want to take the children." She touched Mike's arm. "I saw them at the station when I went to pick up that parcel for you, and I couldn't just leave them there."

"Of course not." Mike bit his lip. "How can we help them?"

"There's only one thing we can do." Kathleen met his eyes. "We need to bring them home with us. There's plenty of room in the extra space we built on."

Mike was silent. He thought of another woman in the home he'd built for Clara, and even though he knew it would only be temporary, the thought squeezed his heart.

"We can't just leave them out here," said Kathleen softly.

Mike let out a break. "Of course not, Ma. I know Pa will agree with you, too." He hesitated. "And you know how I've been needing some help around the general store for a while?"

"Yes." Kathleen's face lit up. "She could be perfect."

"Let's offer her the job and give her a week or so, see how she is," Mike cautioned. "I'm not about to blindly hire a complete stranger."

Kathleen squeezed his arm. "You won't regret it, honey. I know you won't."

Mike let out a long breath as Kathleen bustled over to Selena to give her the good news. "I hope not," he mumbled.

CHAPTER 5

It was amazing how much easier it was to think on a full stomach. Selena smiled brightly at the customer on the other side of the counter. "That'll be two dollars and twelve cents."

The red-haired miner let out a gruff laugh. "You sure do know your arithmetic, miss." He counted out the money and handed it over the counter.

Selena took it and pushed his bag of goods toward him. "Good luck out there. I hear mining's a hard world."

"That it is," the miner agreed, "but we'll all be rich by the end of it. There's got to be more gold on Pike's Peak."

He clumped off, and Selena noted down the transaction in the ledger in quick, tidy handwriting. She kept an eye on the browsing shoppers, taking a seat behind the counter. She could hear Mike walking around in the storeroom behind her as he took stock.

For now, the handful of customers in the store were busy looking at prices and making decisions, and Selena had a rare moment to relax. She didn't know how Mike had run this store for so long without help, even though he'd said that this was always the busiest time of year as everyone stocked up here on the precipice of winter.

She gazed out of the window. Winter might be near, but right now, the world was dry and brown underneath the balmy sunshine. She spotted a familiar figure walking down the street toward the general store and smiled at the sight, rising from her chair.

Kathleen came into the store a few minutes later, Wyatt obediently hanging onto her skirt, Belle on her hip.

"Mama." Belle held out her hands to Selena.

"Hello, honey." Selena took the little girl in her arms and kissed her soft cheek. "Have they been good?" she asked.

"Perfect, as they've been every day this week," said Kathleen, ruffling Wyatt's hair.

The little boy scowled up at her, but his glare was half-hearted.

"I can't begin to thank you enough for looking after them," said Selena. "You've all been so good to me." Tears stung her eyes at the thought.

"Now, now, none of that," said Kathleen comfortably. "Truth be told, I'm having a wonderful time looking after them. They're the most wonderful children." She patted Wyatt's head.

"Can we go to the river now?" Wyatt asked.

"Of course, dearie." Kathleen laughed. "Come on, Bellie-bell. It's time to go."

Belle willingly allowed herself to be handed back over the counter, and Selena felt a knot of tension easing in her heart as she watched the older woman leave with her two kids.

"They're good kids."

Mike's voice must have startled Selena. She spun around, those jade eyes widening as they met his.

"Oh—thank you." She relaxed slightly, smiling. Her smile made two perfect dimples appear in her cheeks.

"And don't feel bad for Ma looking after them." Mike laughed. "She loves them. She's been bored ever since I took over the store—she used to work here with Pa all the time, but now she feels she should stay home and keep an eye on him."

"Is she younger than your father?" Selena asked.

Mike nodded. "By a few years."

"I see." Selena smiled. "You're blessed to have such a tight-knit family."

"Don't I know it," said Mike.

She turned away, and Mike found himself staring at her as she bent over the ledger again. He dropped his eyes, feeling a blush creep to his cheeks.

What are you thinking, Mike? he chided himself inwardly. *She's a widow with two children. What makes you think that you could ever raise another man's children?*

He cleared his throat. "There's something else."

"Yes?" Selena turned to him, her eyes widening. "Is it—about the job?" Her trial period of one week was coming to an end.

"Yes." Mike grinned. "But don't look so worried. You're hardworking and personable. The customers like you, and I —" He cleared his throat. "I like working with you."

Her cheeks flushed slightly.

"The job is yours," Mike said. "For as long as you need it."

"Oh." Selena clasped a hand to her heart, her body sagging with relief. "Oh, Mike, thank you. You don't know what this means to my little family." She was smiling as she looked up at him. "Sometime we'll be able to rent rooms of our own, and—"

"There's no hurry for that either," Mike heard himself say. "We have plenty of room."

Gratitude made her eyes shine even greener. He turned away and hurried back into the storeroom before he could lose himself in them.

Selena worked the broom over the hardwood floor, trying to force herself to keep her eyes on her task. Still, it wasn't easy with Mike restocking shelves just a few feet away.

She couldn't help sneaking a glance across the room. He was lithe and powerful, with broad shoulders; his sleeves were rolled up to the elbow, and strong muscles flexed in his forearms as he lifted cans of peas onto the shelf.

Quickly, Selena turned away, sweeping harder. Mike was one of the most good-looking men she'd ever met. And, as he'd proven when he'd given her the job earlier today, he was kind and generous as well.

She knew he'd been married and become a widower from what Kathleen told him. Maybe he was looking for someone. Maybe...

As her daydream began to run away with her, the front door opened with a jingle of the bell. Selena looked up, surprised. They were about to close the store.

Two women entered, clearly a mother and daughter. The daughter's deep, dark eyes instantly found Mike, and she strode up to him, grinning. "Mike. Hello."

Mike smiled, turning to her. "Hi, Rachel."

The girl beamed at him. "Excited for the winter dance?"

"Oh, Rachel, don't pester him," said the mother. "It's still a month away."

Mike blushed, an adorable expression over his chiseled cheekbones. He lowered his blue-green eyes to the floor. "Yes, I am," he said softly.

"Thank you again for asking me," said Rachel. "It's going to be wonderful."

Selena's heart plummeted. She felt a blush of her own rising to her cheeks and worked the broom more quickly over the floor.

"Are you looking for something?" Mike asked.

"Yes, please," said the mother. "I'm all out of sugar."

They headed for the counter, and Selena paused once more in her sweeping to look up at Mike and Rachel as they walked away. She tried to shake off the absurd disappointment that gripped her.

Mike and Rachel were a very handsome couple. She had no reason to feel the way she did: jealous.

Mike's feet were snug inside the knitted socks Kathleen had made for him. He stretched them out toward the fire, working the stiffness out of his legs and feet as he turned a page in the book he was reading. In the armchair beside his, Joseph had fallen asleep; the old man's head was tipped back, and soft snores emanated from his open mouth.

Kathleen bustled into the room, making Joseph wake up with a snort.

"Oh, sorry, honey." She patted the top of Joseph's head. "I just finished with the dishes. Where's Selena?"

"I think she's still putting the children to bed," said Mike.

"Ah, I see," said Kathleen. "Well, I'm busy making some hot cocoa. If you see her, tell her that I've made some for her, too."

"Will do, Ma," said Mike.

Kathleen bustled off and Joseph fell asleep again, and the rich scent of hot cocoa drifted into the living room. Mike knew it would be accompanied by excellent chocolate chip cookies, but first, he needed the outhouse. He put down his book and headed down the hallway that led to the back door, walking quietly as he passed the room that had once belonged to himself and Clara. Selena and the children slept there—he hadn't set foot in the room since Clara's passing—and he didn't want to wake them.

The children weren't asleep yet. Mike could hear soft voices coming from the bedroom. The door was open just a crack, and warm golden lantern light flooded the hallway as he tiptoed past.

"Thank you, Mama." The voice belonged to Wyatt.

"Shhh, baby," said Selena. "Belle's already asleep. Do you want some more water?"

"No, thank you, Mama." There was a rustle of sheets as the little boy made himself comfortable.

"That's my little boy." Selena kissed him softly. "Sleep well now. They say there'll be snow soon. I'm sure we can build some snowmen. Wouldn't that be nice?"

"Snowmen," Wyatt murmured.

"That's right, baby," said Selena.

The floorboards creaked, and Mike quickened his step, not wanting to be caught eavesdropping.

Wyatt yawned. "Mama?"

Selena stopped. "Yes, honey?"

"I miss Papa." Wyatt's voice was very small.

Mike felt a tug at his heart. He heard Selena hurry back across the floor. "I know, honey," she said. "I miss him too."

"But Papa's not going to come back," said Wyatt. "Is he?"

There was a long silence.

"No, baby." Selena's voice broke. "No, he's not."

"It's not right," Wyatt whispered. "I want a papa again."

"I know you do, honey," said Selena.

"You said we'd have a new papa when we came here," said Wyatt.

For the first time, Mike thought of how confusing and strange it must have been for these children to come all the way to Colorado Territory only for everything to change so abruptly.

"I told you, Wy, things have changed. There's no new papa for you right now. But maybe someday," said Selena again.

Wyatt let out a long sigh. "Mama, isn't Mike going to be our new papa?"

The thought made Mike's heart thump painfully against his chest. He paused by the door and glanced inside. Wyatt was gazing up at his mother, his big blue eyes wide. Selena's face was flushed, and she looked away, turning her eyes to the floor.

"Uh—no, honey." Selena cleared her throat. "For now, you're only going to have a mama, all right?"

Wyatt pulled the covers up to his chin and turned over, his back to his mother. "I just want a papa again," he whispered.

Selena lowered her head, struggling with tears, and Mike's conscience smote him for watching this private scene. He hurried quietly away before anyone could see him.

CHAPTER 6

Late that night, Mike was still wide awake.

He lay in the narrow cot in the room he'd used since his childhood, gazing at the same ceiling. He'd only moved out of this room briefly when he'd been married to Clara. Since then, he'd taken comfort in the boyhood familiarity of the ceiling's boards and the sound of the pine branch against the roof and the view of the mountainside through the chink in the curtains at the window.

Tonight, though, for once, it was not Clara that haunted his mind every time he closed his eyes. It was Wyatt.

He rolled onto his other side and pulled his covers up to his chin. Why couldn't he stop thinking about that little boy with the big, blue eyes?

Isn't Mike going to be our new papa?

Mike closed his eyes tightly. *No, I'm not. I can't be. How could I be a father to two children who aren't my own?* But he thought of Belle's heart-wrenching smile and the way Wyatt ran down the street, yelling with excitement, and somehow, he thought it might not be as hard as he'd expected.

Especially not with their mother's jade-green eyes...

Mike turned over again, letting out a huff of impatience. He could help Wyatt without letting his thoughts run away with him, like a half-broke cayuse with a greenhorn.

Mike understood this might be the last day of sunshine for the year, and since it had fallen on a Sunday afternoon, Kathleen had decided that she was dead set on making the most of it.

The entire family was out in full force on the expanse of dead winter grass above the river. Much of its upper reaches in the mountain had already frozen, and it was a quiet, sluggish trickle down the mountainside, too cold for swimming, but so brilliantly clear that Mike could see the tiny fish flashing in the middle of it. He took advantage of the fish gathering in the warmer waters of the river's lower reaches, his deft fingers quick as he tied a fishing line to a hook and set the pole ready, its line trailing in the water.

His ears were filled with happy conversation. Looking back, he saw that everyone had come for their impromptu post-church picnic. One of Kathleen's big old blankets—the kind that could wrap all the cousins up together—was spread out on the grass. Emma sat contentedly on it, her legs spread out, gently rubbing the slight curve of her belly; beside her, Caleb had his arm around her. Selena sat with Belle on her hip, playing a clapping game with the child. Joseph sat on another corner of the blanket, gazing into the middle distance, his face a picture of vague happiness. Kathleen chattered incessantly with the other women as she unpacked the picnic basket.

It took Mike a moment to realize that he'd mentally included Selena and Belle in his own family group, and the thought made him turn abruptly back to his fishing poles. *You were hardly ready to be a father when Clara talked to you about it,* he told himself. *You're not ready to be a father to two children who aren't even your own.*

His eye caught movement along the dry reeds on the riverbank, and he picked out the huddled little form of Wyatt, perched on a dry old tree stump. The little boy stared sightlessly at the water, swinging his stubby legs so that his heels bumped against the wood.

Mike watched the child for a few moments, sorrow clutching at his heart at the sight of Wyatt's dull, distant expression. He left his fishing pole and walked slowly over to the boy, whistling.

As he approached, Wyatt picked up a little pebble lying beside the stump and tossed it at the river. It splashed loudly into the water.

Mike stopped a few yards away, his thumbs hooked into the belt-loops of his blue jeans. "You've gotta take a smoother one if you want to skip it," he said.

Wyatt gave him a moody look out of those bright blue eyes. He must have gotten them from his father.

"I'm not trying to skip." He pulled his knees up to his chest and rested his chin on them. "I'm just throwing rocks."

"All right." Mike took another step nearer. "Can I throw some, too?"

Wyatt shrugged.

Mike bent and picked up the biggest rock he could find. Using both hands, he hurled it into the river as hard as he could. It landed with a giant splash, and Wyatt sat up straighter, a giggle escaping him despite himself. Mike hadn't heard him giggle much lately, and the sound was startlingly melodic.

"Like that?" Mike asked.

Wyatt's laugh grew louder. "Like that." He paused. "Can you teach me to skip?"

"Sure." Mike winked at him. "Did you know that I'm the skipping champion of Mine's Place?"

Wyatt gave him a suspicious look. "Really?"

Mike scoffed. "No."

Wyatt laughed again, and Mike grinned back easily. It felt so effortless with him.

He bent down and picked up one of the smooth stones, turning it over and over in his hand. Then he threw it with an expert little flick of his wrist. The stone skipped magnificently, hopping along the water six, seven, eight times before it plopped back into the water.

"Whoa." Wyatt jumped to his feet. "Show me?"

Mike spent the next ten minutes showing the boy how to pick a flat, smooth stone, and how to throw it so that it spun wildly and just kissed the surface of the slow-moving river a few times before it landed. Wyatt tried again and again, but by the fourth attempt, the pebble still refused to skip and fell into the water.

"I'm no good." Wyatt turned away, his cheeks flushing. "I'm no good at anything."

Mike stared at the boy, shocked. "No, Wyatt, that's just not true. You're just learning, is all. You'll have it in a minute."

"I'm *no good* at anything." Wyatt sniffed loudly.

"No, you're good at many things," said Mike. "Look how nicely you help your mother and Mrs. Keating around the house."

"I can do *girl* things," said Wyatt scornfully. "My mama showed me all the girl things. But I can't do boy things." He looked up at Mike, and his eyes were wet. "Man things. My papa never got to teach me."

Mike felt his heart crack. He put his hand on Wyatt's little shoulder. "Well, how about I teach you, then?" he said. "But you can't just give up. You've got to keep trying."

Wyatt's face brightened just a little. "All right."

They walked back to the riverbank, and this time, Wyatt chose a perfectly smooth flat stone. And when he threw it, it skipped and skipped and skipped until the little boy's laughter came up from deep down inside his belly.

Selena looked around, startled. She hadn't heard Wyatt make that sound in a long, long time.

Not since John died, she realized.

"Where's Wyatt?" she asked, looking around. Belle giggled and clutched at her hands, still wanting to play.

"Over there," said Kathleen calmly. "With Mike."

Selena looked in the direction Kathleen was pointing. When she peered through the rushes, she spotted her small son standing beside Mike's lithe figure. For a moment, her eyes dwelled on Mike. He was wearing blue jeans, as usual, and heavy boots; his shirt was pale blue, and he'd rolled up the sleeves to show his brawny forearms.

Beside him, Wyatt was tiny, but his laughter filled Selena's entire world. She watched as he bent and picked up a stone, then showed it to Mike. Mike nodded in approval. Wyatt pulled back his arm and flicked the stone toward the river. It bounced twice, then fell into the water with a *plop*.

"That's all right." said Mike cheerfully. He picked up another. "Just try again."

Wyatt skipped the stone with enthusiasm, laughing in delight when it skipped four times.

"That's it." Mike laughed, the sound deep and booming. "That's my boy."

Selena looked away, her eyes stinging with tears. *That's my boy.* John used to say that to Wyatt all the time, and she didn't think he'd heard those words in that joyous tone since John's death.

"Selena?" said Emma gently beside her. "Are you alright?"

"I'm all right." She managed a smile. "I just haven't seen Wyatt so happy for so long, and I have your family to thank for it."

"Of course, dear." Kathleen patted Selena's shoulder. "You've been wonderful for us, too. I'm so glad that Mike has more help around the store now."

"Oh, Kathleen, I know I hardly even earn my keep at the store. You've all been so kind to us," said Selena.

Kathleen met her eyes, and for once, the older woman's gaze was very serious.

"You said you haven't seen Wyatt so happy for a long time," she said softly. "Well, my son hasn't been this happy in years, either. Your family makes Michael light up. I would do anything to see him like this."

Joseph grunted in agreement.

Selena looked up at Mike and Wyatt again. They were walking back toward the fishing poles, talking. She watched how Wyatt hung his thumbs in his belt-loops, just like Mike was doing, and couldn't help smiling.

"You and your two children have been good for our family already," said Kathleen softly. "I have no doubt that you will only continue to be better and better for us."

Selena gave her a surprised look. "What do you mean by that, Kathleen?"

The older woman let out a low chuckle, her eyes twinkling. "Oh, I think we'll find out."

CHAPTER 7

Selena hummed to herself as she scrubbed the floor on her hands and knees. The pressure of the hardwood on her skin was annoying at times, but there was so much satisfaction in seeing its shine return as she scrubbed. She dipped her brush back in the bucket, grateful that the water was lukewarm, and started on a fresh patch of floor.

"Need a coffee break?" Mike asked, leaning over the counter to peer at her where she scrubbed.

She smiled up at him. "That would be great. I'll make the coffee. Do we have enough time before we open the store? I just want to finish this floor before the customers arrive."

"You're nearly done. I'm sure we have time," said Mike.

Selena went behind the counter to the cast-iron coal stove that heated the store. The enamel kettle still had some water in it, so she put it on the stove and reached for two mugs from the nearby cabinet.

"Let's try some of those new coffee beans that came on the train," Mike suggested.

Selena laughed. "I thought you said those were for the customers."

Mike's eyes sparkled. "Well, we have to do some quality control, don't we?"

Selena laughed again, surprised at how easy it was to laugh in Mike's presence. She pressed her lips together. *What are you doing? He's in love with Rachel. Don't look at him like that.*

Mike didn't seem to notice the hot blush on her cheeks. He'd already turned away and was paging through the ledger, checking yesterday's transactions.

"I have to thank you, Selena," he said.

"Thank me?" asked Selena. "What on earth would you have to thank me for? Your family is the one who's saving mine."

Mike looked over his shoulder, smiling. "Thank you for being good company in the store. You don't know what it means to me, to have someone around—and not just for all your hard work, either." He cleared his throat, and his ears were reddening. "I like having you around."

Selena's blush deepened. "I—I like being around," she managed. *I like you*, she wanted to say. *I like the way you play with my children and the way you're unfailingly kind to every person who comes into the shop and the way you make me laugh so effortlessly.*

She pushed the thought away, reminding herself again of Rachel as she went into the storeroom for a bag of the new coffee beans. When she came back into the storefront, she began to grind them, and their delicious smell filled the air.

"Mmm, the customers are going to love that," said Mike.

"I think so too." Selena blushed again; the word *love* sounded so fantastic when he said it. "So, uh, you must be excited for the winter dance. It's just a couple of days away."

"So it is." Mike shook his head. "I can't believe it's December already."

"Time flies when you're having fun," Selena blurted out.

Mike's eyes met hers. "Yes... yes, it sure does." He leaned against the counter. "Yes, I suppose I'm excited enough. Are you going?"

"No one asked me," Selena admitted, "but Kathleen invited me anyway, so I'll be there. I'm a little nervous, to be honest."

"Nervous?" said Mike. "Why?"

"Because I haven't gone out dancing at all since marrying John seven years ago," said Selena. "You could say that it's been a while."

Mike inclined his head. "For me, too," he admitted. He folded his arms, staring down at the floor. "It... took a long time for me even to be able to think of dancing with another woman, after Clara."

His late wife's name came out a little strangled, and Selena was silent for a respectful few moments as she poured the coffee. She handed Mike his cup. "I'm sorry. I have an idea of how that feels."

"I know." Mike took his coffee. "Thank you."

"I think it's brave of you to try again," said Selena. "I don't think I could ever have been brave enough to take the first step if it wasn't for the fact that my children need a father."

Mike gave her a quick, sideways glance. She couldn't quite work out what it meant.

"It was my mother who talked me into it," he said. "She reminded me that this is what Clara would have wanted." He looked away, dragging a sleeve across his eyes. "She's right. Clara is happy now. There's no reason why I can't try to be, too, even if I'll carry her with me in my heart forever."

"I don't think we ever stop grieving," Selena agreed. "But we can still live our lives, grief and all."

He met her eyes; his lashes were slightly damp, but he smiled. "That's it," he said. "That's exactly right."

Their eyes held each other, and Selena couldn't look away. She felt a sudden longing to know what it would feel like for Mike's arms to be wrapped around her. She wanted to lean her head into his chest and feel the rhythmic thump of his heart. Instead, she reached out and brushed a hand lightly over his shoulder.

"Well, whoever you end up with, I know you're going to be a wonderful father to your children someday," she said.

His eyes widened in surprise. "Do you think so?"

"Yes, of course." Selena forced herself to take a step back and sipped her coffee, breaking eye contact. "Haven't you noticed the change in Wyatt since you've been spending so much time with him? I can't thank you enough for all the attention you give him. My little boy is completely different, Mike. He's so much more like the child I had before John died."

Mike's shoulders relaxed slightly. "That's... very good news. I've never spent much time with children before."

"You haven't?" Selena raised her eyebrows. "I would never have guessed it. You're so good with them. And Belle loves you, too, of course."

Mike let out his rumbling laugh. "It's impossible not to love Belle. She's so precious."

"Until she has one of her tantrums," said Selena, and they both laughed.

Their laughter wrapped around each other, the high notes of hers fitting perfectly against the low notes of his, and she had to force herself to look away and stop laughing. Stop her heart from running away with her as it dreamed of Mike seeing Belle and Wyatt as his own.

The church hall was packed. It was the biggest building in Mine's Place, yet the simple space was filled with the entire community, delighted to distract themselves from the growing cold with an evening of fellowship, music, and laughter. Long tables lined the walls, rich with the finest harvest feast, and people milled around the tables, their bursts of laughter rising against the scraping music from the little band in the back corner. The saloon band bravely scratched a merry tune from their old instruments, and Mrs. Spencer accompanied them on her celeste, which was propped up against the back corner.

Everyone was happy, and everything Mike smelled and saw was good. But he couldn't push away the discontentment clawing at his heart.

"Listen to Mama." said Rachel. "Isn't she good?"

Mike forced a smile as Rachel hung on his arm. He wished she wouldn't cling to him like this. "She's very good," he managed.

Rachel laughed. "Wait until you hear her play 'Old Dan Tucker'. That'll fill this dance floor."

It already looked full to Mike. The people of Mine's Place were all in their Sunday best, and their boots clopped and thudded on the wooden floor as they danced. Men were freshly shaven, some for the first time in months; women wore their hair in loose, flowing styles, the collars of their dresses starched to brilliant white. A whole collection of people was on the dance floor, from elderly couples who spun and hopped stiffly, to teenagers giggling and clutching each other in giddy excitement.

"Are you hungry?" Mike asked, shifting his arm a little to loosen Rachel's grip.

She tightened her fingers. "No, not yet. Let's dance."

Reluctantly, Mike allowed himself to be towed out onto the dance floor just as the tune on the celeste changed. Rachel laughed, delighted, and turned to face him. She rested a hand on his shoulder and clutched his left hand. "I love this song." she said. "'The Arkansas Traveler'."

The beat was cheerful and easy to follow, at least, and Mike found himself stomping across the floor with Rachel in his arms. She giggled and blushed and hung onto him, and he began to wish that she'd grow tired of dancing. But song after song filled the hall, and Rachel's energy only seemed to grow.

Mike piloted her across the floor slowly, wishing that the plodding rendition of "Fare You Well Polly" would come to an end, when the church hall door opened in a sudden gust of cool air. It slammed quickly, sealing them once again in warmth, and Mike glanced up at it.

And Selena was there.

Mike's breath caught in his chest. She was wearing a new dress—he'd seen her working on it a few times in the past two weeks—of a sturdy green cotton that made her jade eyes stand out even more. Her auburn hair flowed over her shoulders, soft and free, and as she looked around the room, her eyes found his. Her lips twitched up in a smile that clutched at his heart.

Mike's foot descended sharply onto Rachel's toe.

"Ouch." Rachel squealed, jumping back. "Mike, watch out."

"Sorry—sorry." Mike forced his attention back to Rachel. "Sorry."

"What were you looking at?" Rachel asked, raising an eyebrow.

Mike cleared his throat. "Nothing. I just got distracted by the door opening, that's all."

Rachel giggled, her eyes softening. "The door opened? I didn't notice." She hesitated, her cheeks turning very pink. "I haven't noticed anything but you all night."

Mike blinked, surprised by her forwardness. Then again, he realized, he was the one who'd approached her first.

"Let's stop and get something to drink," he suggested.

"Oh, all right," said Rachel as the song came to an end. "I suppose we can do that."

They made their way to the table where ginger ale was being served, and Mike tried his best to keep his attention on the ale instead of on Selena. He sneaked a sideways glance at her where she was leaning against the wall, chatting with Emma. How come the entire hall wasn't staring at her? She was impossible not to look at. It was as though a star had fallen from the night sky and now glowed amid the rest of the community.

"Are you alright?" Rachel asked. "You've gone very quiet."

"Oh, I'm fine," said Mike hastily. He smiled at her. "Ginger ale?"

They stood by the table, sipping together, and Rachel prattled on incessantly about nothing that caught Mike's interest. He tried to look into her eyes and smile and nod, but every now and then, a flash of green eyes or a glimmer of auburn hair would catch his attention. He couldn't help noticing when Tommy Green, who was a nice enough young man, asked Selena to dance. She said yes, and when she laid her hand in his, a strange, bitterly cold feeling rose from the pit of Mike's stomach.

He put down his empty glass and took Rachel's hand. "Come on. Let's jump in with the next song."

It was a slower song, its gentle beat leading the dancers in soft arcs around the floor. Mike forced himself to train his eyes on Rachel, even when Selena and Tommy skimmed by; he just caught the edge of Selena's laugh as she went by.

You're going insane, Mike told himself angrily. *You're dancing with a sweet young woman—one who could give you your own children.*

He smiled at Rachel. "This is fun."

"Yes." Rachel grinned up at him. "It's amazing."

"How's your older brother?" Mike asked, desperate to make some kind of conversation.

"Connor? Oh, he's fine. His little girl was just born. He's always sending me letters from Utah," said Rachel.

"That's nice. You must be excited to be an aunt," said Mike.

Rachel shrugged.

He frowned, surprised by her reaction. "Don't you and Connor get along?"

"Oh, yes. We do. And we visit every Christmas," said Rachel. "I just—well, I guess I haven't thought of myself as an aunt yet." She laughed. "I hardly think about myself as more than a girl."

Mike looked at her. "Haven't you thought of having children of your own?"

Silence stretched between them, and they moved across the dance floor automatically. For the first time all night, Rachel's smile faded, and she looked away.

"Children could be helpful on the farm, I guess," she said.

Mike said nothing. But the sinking feeling in the pit of his stomach only continued to grow.

CHAPTER 8

Selena smiled at Lawrence Thomas, a nice young man with a thatch of red hair. "Thank you. That was fun," she said, slightly breathless.

Lawrence gave her an oddly formal little bow. "Anytime, ma'am." He let go of her hand and disappeared into the crowd. Probably in search of food, Selena guessed, and the thought of food made her stomach rumble. She was ready for dinner herself.

Her eyes skimmed across the dance floor as Mrs. Spencer struck up another lively tune on the celeste. She tried to stop herself, but it was far too easy to spot Mike twirling Rachel across the dance floor. The sight of another woman in his arms made something strange flow through her blood, something that was hot and cold all at once. She tried to get a closer look at his face, to see if he was really enjoying it, but forced herself to look away. *That's none of your business, Selena,* she chided herself.

She turned and picked her way through the crowd to a table where a cheerful old woman was dishing up gigantic slices of pumpkin pie. Selena took one and thanked her.

"Selena." said Emma's familiar voice. "Over here."

Selena looked up. Emma leaned against the wall a few feet away, beckoning and grinning.

She was grateful to see a familiar face. Although she'd mostly managed to distract herself from Mike by dancing with a few other men this evening, Emma would be an even better distraction. She made her way over to the pregnant woman and smiled at her. "Shouldn't you be dancing with Caleb?"

Emma laughed. "Between you and me, I don't quite have the energy that I used to." She touched her belly, which was mostly hidden underneath her loose dress. "But I was about to ask you the same thing—about dancing with my brother."

Selena's cheeks burned. "Your brother? I—I don't know what you mean."

"I think you do," said Emma.

Selena stared down at her pumpkin pie. "Emma, I… I mean, he's with Rachel. And she'll be a perfect woman for him."

Emma scoffed. "That girl? Don't make me laugh. Oh, Rachel's lovely, but she's far too young for Mike. He needs a mature woman, someone who can stand with him when times grow hard." She gave Selena a pointed look.

Selena's blush deepened. She shoved a forkful of pumpkin pie into her mouth before she could say anything foolish, although she feared her blush was already giving her away. Judging by Emma's chuckle, she was right.

She picked at the pumpkin pie until Mrs. Spencer and the band struck up with a new song. This time it was something older: "On Springfield Mountain," a ballad she'd heard often in Boston. Its soft tones made it one of her favorites, and as she looked up to see if someone might dance with her, she found herself looking right into Mike's eyes.

"Hello, Selena." It sounded like his mouth was dry.

Selena nearly choked on her pumpkin pie. She managed to avoid spraying crumbs everywhere, put down the fork, and smiled up at Mike. "Hello," she squeaked.

"I was wondering." Mike rubbed the back of his neck. "Um, if you'd want to dance with me."

Selena stared up at him. *Yes. Yes, I want to dance with you. More than anything in the world, I want to dance with you right now.* She almost shouted it, but instead, she began to ask, "Where's R—"

Emma's foot tapped sharply against her shin.

"I mean." Selena cleared her throat. "I mean, yes please."

Mike smiled, the expression sudden and brilliant as only he could make it. "Wonderful." He held out an arm.

Emma took Selena's plate out of her hands. She glanced at Emma, who gave her an enormous grin and jerked her head toward the dance floor.

Part of Selena wondered if she was making a ridiculous mistake. The other part, the rest of her, knew there was nothing else to do other than wrapping an arm around Mike's and allowing him to lead her out onto the dance floor. When she turned to face him, their hands found one another unbidden. She rested her free hand on his shoulder, and somehow it fit there. Somehow it felt as though they'd done this before.

They swayed to the gentle music, and Selena told herself that all would be well as long as she didn't look up into Mike's eyes. She stared at his bolo tie instead. It was held with a bright silver clasp, and she forced herself to stare at it.

"I love this song," said Mike.

"Me too. It's one of the oldest songs I've ever known," said Selena.

"What's it about?" asked Mike. "It sounds…" He cleared his throat. "Romantic."

Selena chuckled. "Well, almost. It's about a young man who's bitten by a snake, so he goes to a beautiful girl, who sucks out the poison."

"Gruesome," Mike mused. His breath rumbled through his chest as he spoke. "Still romantic."

"Not really. She has a rotten tooth, and they both die," said Selena.

"I didn't expect that," said Mike, and burst into his rolling laughter.

Selena couldn't resist. She looked up into his eyes, and the sparkle in them was enough to make her laugh with him. Enough to make her forget all the reasons why she shouldn't be dancing with Mike Keating, and just throw herself into this single perfect moment.

The snow came down in fat, white flakes, thick and profuse as it pattered gently on the roof of the general store. Notebook in hand, Selena gazed out of the storeroom's window. Somehow the snow out here was different than it had been in Boston. Bostonian snow had been picturesque for a few brief hours after settling on the rooftops and roadsides, but quickly turned into a yellow-gray slush after the city's pollution and traffic reached it.

Here, the snow was the most brilliant white that Selena had ever seen. Filtering down out of a low, gray sky, it was so pure and clear that every snowflake could have been carved from a diamond. Where it settled on the mountainside, it formed a carpet of perfect white, unmarred even by the footprints of a stray dog or a pigeon.

"Quite something, huh?" a deep voice rumbled from the other side of the storeroom.

Selena grinned over at Mike. He leaned over a shelf, counting cans of corned beef.

"It's special," she said. "Snow just doesn't look like this in the city."

"Wait till the children wake up tomorrow morning and find themselves in a wonderland," said Mike. "I'm guessing there'll be clear skies tomorrow, so they'll be able to come out and play in it."

"They'll love that." said Selena. She shook her head. "Last winter, they couldn't go outside at all. I just…" She blushed. "I didn't have warm enough clothes that fit them."

Mike looked up at her, and their eyes met. "Well, now everything is different," he said softly. "They have coats and scarves and mittens, and they're going to have a wonderful time."

Selena smiled. "Thank you."

"Why are you thanking me?" Mike chuckled. "You bought them those things."

"I did, but you made it possible. And more than that, you..." She hesitated. "You have a way of drawing me out of my past and reminding me that the present is far more wonderful."

Mike's smile reached down deep into the pit of her soul. It called to something inside her, something that had lain dormant for a long time. Selena forced herself to look away, her mind whirling with questions. It had been two days since the dance, since they'd spent the rest of that evening twirling and laughing on the floor, even after Mrs. Spencer had left with Rachel in a fury. The saloon band had still played, and as long as they'd played, Mike and Selena had danced.

Then, yesterday had been busy, and there had hardly been a minute to talk. Until now, in the silence of the storeroom, with the store closed and stock taking in progress, just the two of them. The thought made Selena's heart flutter madly in her chest.

"Thanks for helping me take stock." Mike broke the silence. "We have forty-five cans of corned beef."

"Of course," said Selena, writing down the number in her notebook. "I couldn't leave you to do this all on your own. It's a late night for us both already."

"It is," said Mike. His voice softened. "I'm glad you're here. I like your company."

She looked up at him. It was the first time he'd said anything about how he felt about her since the dance.

She couldn't stop herself from saying it. "I like your company, too. More than you know."

Mike's eyes held hers. "You do?"

"Yes," Selena whispered.

He took a few steps nearer to her, and her heart fluttered wildly in her chest. She felt like a girl again, giddy with his closeness as he stopped just a foot away from her.

"Selena…" He reached out, wrapped his hand around hers.

The notebook and pencil clattered out of her numb fingers. She couldn't look anywhere except into his eyes, and she searched them, questioning the reason for their deep, joyous glow.

"Yes?" she breathed.

He opened his mouth as if to speak, but no words would come. Instead, he pulled her a little closer, leaned down, and kissed her as she had not been kissed since John died. Perhaps even before John died. And then all thoughts of John left her mind, and all that was left was Mike's soft touch as his arms wrapped around her body, and the way his hair felt against her fingers when she wrapped her hands around his neck, and the soft explorations of his lips against her own, tender and certain.

When they pulled apart, Selena's heart was singing a single long note of joy, and she couldn't stop staring into his eyes. His hands pressed against her back, still holding her closer.

His lips parted again, and for a moment she thought he would give her another kiss, and her heart cried out for it. Then, two pink spots appeared in his cheeks. He suddenly let go of her and stepped back.

"I think that's enough for tonight," he croaked. "I—I'll put out the stove."

He pulled away from her and disappeared into the storefront, and Selena was left alone in the storeroom, with no idea of what to make of his kiss or his words or his sudden departure.

They left the general store and walked toward the house in total silence.

It was bitterly cold. Mike could tell Selena was freezing despite her layers of coats; the tip of her perfect little button nose was bright red, and she had her arms wrapped around herself as they walked. It was still snowing, and the snowflakes settled in tiny bright stars on Selena's glorious, flowing hair, a splash of brilliant color among the grays and whites of winter.

He thought of a thousand things to say, but all of them sounded foolish to his own ears. Should he apologize for kissing her? Yet he wasn't sorry, not unless he'd frightened or hurt her somehow. In that moment, as she'd kissed him, it had seemed as though she'd enjoyed it as much as he did.

But then she had stared up at him, trembling, and he couldn't understand why she trembled. Panic had overwhelmed him, and he'd dashed out of the room.

What had he done? Was she angry? Was she afraid of him? Had he crossed a line?

Mike simply didn't know. So, he said nothing, and neither did Selena. They walked all the way back home in silence through the falling snow.

CHAPTER 9

The customer who staggered into the store was so covered in snow that Selena didn't recognize him until he pulled off his Stetson, shaking the snow off the hat and through the door before closing it behind him. It was Caleb, Mike's friendly brother-in-law, and his shoulders were thickly dusted with snow. He clumped across the store to the counter and smiled at Selena.

"Afternoon," he grunted. "It's a wild one out there."

"It must be." said Selena. "We've had hardly any customers all day, and Mike's had to shovel the snow twice." She sneezed.

Caleb gave her a concerned look. "You alright?"

"Oh, yes. I'm fine," said Selena, even though the truth was that her heart felt shredded inside her, something which bothered her far more than the tickle in her throat.

She glanced over her shoulder to the storeroom. Mike was inside, gathering ropes to hang in the display window. She didn't think he'd spoken ten words to her today, and those words had only been brusque instructions.

It had been the same for the three days since the kiss that she could still feel lingering on her lips when she dreamed.

"You look a little flushed, is all," said Caleb.

"It's nice and warm in here, compared to outside," Selena reassured him. "How can I help you?"

"I just came to pick up some extra flour and sugar. They're saying we'll have heavy snowfalls for the next few days, and I want to make sure we have everything we need at home." Caleb grinned. "Now that Emma's eating for two, you know."

Selena laughed. "I'm sure she's very grateful to you."

She weighed out the flour and sugar, trying to ignore the faint cold sweat that kept trickling down the sides of her face. She brushed it away with her sleeve and handed Caleb his bag of flour, then bent to scoop out sugar from the burlap bag at her feet. When she straightened, brief dizziness gripped her, and she staggered, grasping the counter to steady herself.

"Are you sure you're alright?" said Caleb, frowning at her.

"Fine. Quite fine," Selena panted. "Will that be all?"

Caleb paid for his goods and left, casting a last, nervous glance over his shoulder before he left the store.

There were no other customers, and total silence settled over the store. Selena sat down on the stool behind the counter and glanced out of the window at the falling snow. Was it cold outside? It felt warm here.

Yet that didn't worry her, not now. All she could think of now was the throbbing of her heart.

Mike clumped past her, carrying a bunch of lariats. He didn't even look at her as he walked across the storefront and went to hang them in the window to display his new stock to nearby ranchers. She watched his quick, competent movements, his ease as he worked, and her heart was filled with a deep longing to see him smile at her again. To have him look into her eyes again.

She dragged her eyes away, hurting and furious with herself. Had she led him on? Had she failed him somehow? What if he threw her out of his home for whatever wrong she'd committed? Where would she go with her children in this snow?

Berating herself, she pushed aside her broken heart, got to her feet, and grabbed her feather duster to clean the windowsills. She would prove herself a good worker. She would keep her distance. Then, maybe, hopefully, the safety of her children would at least be secured.

Selena let out a low, hacking cough. It had a nasty, bubbling edge to it, and Mike couldn't help looking up from the lariats in his hand. She'd gone over to the window, and she worked her feather duster over the sill even though she'd cleaned them all only yesterday.

He noticed the bright pink spots in her cheeks and his heart squeezed in his chest. She didn't look well. She should be at home, in bed, where it was warm. But how could he tell her that? How could he say anything to her? He'd ruined everything by kissing her.

Miserable, Mike turned back to the lariats, cursing himself for wronging her. He'd thought the kiss was what she wanted, but he'd been wrong. He had botched his one chance at what might have been real love, and he'd caused her misery instead. He hated himself for it.

Selena let out a soft sound, almost a whimper. Mike looked up, and his heart skipped inside his chest. She was trembling, leaning against the windowsill, and her cheeks were suddenly ashen.

The room was spinning helplessly around Selena. She clutched at the windowsill, the feather duster clattering out of her fingers, desperate to make it stop. But the spinning just went faster and faster.

She tried to call for help, but the only sound to escape her lips was a soft whimper, and the spinning wouldn't stop. Her fingers grew senseless on the windowsill, and the floor tipped wildly under her feet.

She knew two more things before darkness claimed her: the thump of her body striking the wooden floor, and Mike's voice, calling her name.

"Selena."

Mike ran toward her where she lay stretched on the floor, motionless. His heart fluttered in his chest as he fell to his knees beside her. She was so pale, and except for the faint twitching of her chest as she took shallow, rasping breaths, she didn't move.

"Selena?" Mike whispered.

She made no response. Mike reached out and gently gripped her hand, and her skin was blazing hot to the touch. His heart stuttered within him.

The bell over the shop door chimed, and boots clumped on the wood. "Would you believe it," Caleb said sheepishly, "I forgot to get—" He stopped. "Mike? What's happened?"

Mike looked up, aware that his eyes were filling with tears and too afraid to be ashamed of them. "Run," he croaked. "Run and get the doctor, Caleb. Something's wrong. Something's very wrong."

Caleb's eyes widened. He said not a word, just turned and sprinted out of the store, the door swinging shut behind him.

Mike slid his arms under Selena and scooped her into his arms. Her head lolled helplessly against his shoulder, and he nearly cried out at the pang of fear that pierced his heart. Her soft hair trailed over his arm, but even that seemed dull and lifeless now.

"You're going to be all right, Selena," he croaked, striding to the door. "You're going to be all right."

But he didn't know that to be true. All he knew was that Clara, too, had been this pale.

Mike paced up and down in the hallway outside Selena's room that had once been his, just as he had done on that awful day three years ago. He couldn't help himself. The floorboards creaked with every step he took, and his tortured mind roiled like boiling water.

He had wronged her, and now he was going to lose her. How could this be happening?

He reached the end of the hall, pivoted on his heel, paced back across the floor. There was a voice from inside the room. Mike stopped, trembling, and listened. He thought he heard the rumble of Dr. Vickers' voice, but was that Selena responding?

The front door crashed open. "Michael, honey?" It was Kathleen.

"Ma." Mike's eyes blurred with tears. He blinked them back and hurried into the kitchen, where his mother was pulling off her mittens and unwinding her scarf from around her neck.

"Oh, baby, how is she?" Kathleen asked, rushing over to him and wrapping him in a warm hug.

"I don't know, Ma." Mike held her closer. "I don't know. Doc's still in there with her. Pa's in his room. Where are the children?"

"I left them with Emma. They don't need to see their mother like this," said Kathleen. "I'm only glad Caleb came to fetch me while I was visiting with Anna, or I wouldn't even have known anything was amiss."

"Caleb was wonderful. He went for Doc while I was with Selena." The sound of her name made Mike's voice break.

"Oh, honey." Kathleen took his hand and squeezed it firmly. "Sit yourself down. I'm going to make some hot coffee, and then everything will look a little better."

Mike sank down on a chair at the kitchen table and stared at nothing. "I feel so helpless," he croaked. "I don't know what to do for her."

"There's one thing you can always, always do, honey." Kathleen put a hand on his shoulder. "You can pray."

Mike, trembling, lowered his head. He had no words for how afraid he was, so he offered up his sheer terror instead, praying that he would still be understood.

Footsteps creaked on the wooden floor.

"Doctor," said Kathleen. "How is she?"

Mike raised his head. Dr. Vickers was tall and stooping, with a handlebar mustache, and his face was grim as he set his box of medicines down on the kitchen table.

"It's a bad cold, Mrs. Keating," he said, "very bad. Her fever is very high."

Mike trembled in his chair. "Is it the same as—" He couldn't finish.

"Not yet, young man." Dr. Vickers offered him a compassionate smile. "She's young and strong, and she has a fighting chance yet, but she'll need nursing and plenty of rest. If we can get her fever under control, she'll do just fine."

Mike squeezed his eyes tight shut. The doctor had said the same thing about Clara, but her fever had run wildly out of control, no matter what Mike, Joseph, Kathleen, and Emma did. All their efforts had been useless.

"Try not to despair, Mr. Keating." Dr. Vickers put a big hand on his shoulder. "I will be back in the morning. Here, Mrs. Keating. This medicine will help for the fever; have her drink it morning and night, if she can sit up and swallow."

"Thank you, doctor," said Kathleen.

Then Dr. Vickers was gone, and Kathleen put a cup of coffee on the table in front of Mike, who simply stared at it.

"All right, honey. We'll be all right," she said. "Whatever the Good Lord wills, it's going to happen. Whatever that is, it's always for our good. You know that."

"I know," Mike whispered. "I'm just scared."

"Then it's a good thing that He is with you now, dear." Kathleen kissed the top of his head. "Emma will take care of the children. I'll look after Selena, and she'll be just fine."

Mike looked up at her. "I want to care for Selena," he said, almost before knowing what he wanted to say.

Kathleen blinked at him, a poorly hidden smile tugging at her lips. "You do?"

"Yes," said Mike. "I'll look after Selena. I'll ask Caleb to watch the store. I'm sure he won't mind."

"He won't mind a bit, honey," said Kathleen. "As soon as the snow stops, I'll go and ask him. No one's going to come to the store in this weather, anyway."

Mike nodded. He got to his feet and reached for a pail. He'd sponge Selena's face and arms with cool water, and he'd be ready with sips of sweet tea if she woke. He knew what to do because he had done it all before.

And he kept praying that, this time, the outcome would be different.

CHAPTER 10

Mike's back ached sharply. His eyelids fluttered, and he stirred, wincing at the pressure of the chair digging into the small of his back.

The chair. He sat up with a gasp. He'd fallen asleep while caring for Selena, and the thought terrified him. Panic lanced through him as he looked down at her motionless form. She was paler than she had been when he'd fallen asleep, and her auburn hair was a cloud around her head, deep circles under her eyes. For a long second, Mike thought the worst. Then he saw her chest stir as she breathed.

He let out a breath. "It's all right, Selena," he whispered, reaching for the pail of water beside him.

He'd lost track of the time. He had no idea how long he'd spent here at her bedside, nibbling at the sandwiches

Kathleen brought to him, sleeping in fitful snatches beside her bed. Selena, too, drifted in and out of consciousness. Sometimes she could whisper a few coherent words of thanks as he sponged her face and arms. Sometimes she would cry out and thrash in fever dreams that left her worn out and terrified, sobbing as Mike brushed her hair away from her face and spoke soothing words that he wasn't sure she could hear.

Now, though, she seemed peaceful, and Mike's heart froze within him. Clara had also seemed peaceful, right before—

He couldn't let himself think of that. Instead, he leaned forward and wrapped his hand around Selena's limp fingers. "Selena?" he whispered.

Her fingers twitched in his. Her eyes fluttered open, and for a moment their breathtaking jade looked up at him. "Mike," she murmured. "I feel... I feel better." Then her eyes closed again, and she sank back against her pillows.

Mike let out a long breath as he realized that her fingers were cool and dry in his hand. He pressed the back of his hand to her forehead, and the blazing heat had gone. Her breathing was free and easy, slow and measured.

The door creaked open, and Kathleen peered into the room. "How is she, dear?"

"Ma, I—" Mike stared up at her. "I think she's better."

Kathleen hurried into the room and felt Selena's forehead. When she looked up at Mike, she was grinning from ear to ear. "Michael, darling, the fever's gone. Look how peacefully she's sleeping." She let out a soft laugh. "She's all right, honey. She's going to be just fine."

Mike lowered his head, trembling, and let out a silent prayer of thanksgiving. When he raised his head, he couldn't be ashamed of the tears running down his cheeks. He rubbed his thumb over the back of Selena's hand, staring at her as she slept. He had never seen anything so beautiful. Never.

"Ma." He looked up at Kathleen. "Can you watch her for a little while? There's something I must do."

"What is it, dear?" asked Kathleen.

"I have to go speak to Rachel." He took a deep breath. "I think it's only right."

Kathleen's eyes sparkled. "You do?"

"Yes." Mike squared his shoulders. "Can you care for Selena, please?"

"Of course, dear." Kathleen grinned widely. "You go do what you need to do."

The door swung open as soon as Mike knocked, and Mrs. Spencer glared at him from inside the farmhouse. He spotted her celeste standing in the corner of the kitchen, and his toes curled.

"What do you want?" Mrs. Spencer demanded.

Mike swallowed. "Hello, Mrs. Spencer. I was wondering if, uh, if I could speak with Rachel."

Mrs. Spencer grunted. "About time, young man." She jerked her head. "She's in the barn, helping her father."

"Thank you, ma'am," said Mike, but the door slammed shut in his face before he could finish speaking.

He sighed. Leaving his tired horse tied to a hitching rail, Mike trudged through knee-deep snow to the barn opposite the house on the Spencers' property. When he pushed the door open, it was blissfully warm inside after the bitter cold of the wintry day.

Rachel was in the tack stall, cleaning the plow horse's harness. Mike felt a pang of guilt as he stepped inside. She hummed to herself as she worked, and he wished he'd never caused her all this trouble.

"Rachel?" he managed.

She turned around, her eyes widening at the sight of him. "Mike." She wrung her rag in her hands. "I didn't expect to see you here again."

Mike shoved his hands into the pockets of his jeans. "There's something I need to tell you."

Rachel's eyes narrowed. "What?" she asked.

He squared his shoulders. "I wanted to apologize for the way I acted at the dance the other day. It wasn't right. I shouldn't have given you the impression that I did."

Rachel's shoulders relaxed, and a smile returned to her face. "Oh, Mike, thank you for coming here and saying that. I was so afraid after you suddenly went off and danced with that lady who works in your store. I thought—well, I thought you didn't even care for me anymore."

Mike took a deep breath and said what he had come to say. And Rachel's yelling pursued him all the way out of the barn and back onto his horse, her furious cries making his ears tingle.

Strong fingers were wrapped around Selena's hand, a callused thumb gently caressing the back of her hand. It was a tender touch, gentle and generous, and Selena let out a long sigh of contentment at the sensation.

It had been a long time since she'd felt such love.

But wait. Where was that love coming from? The hand was too callused to be Kathleen's. Vague scraps of memory came to her, swimming up from a mind dazed by fever dreams over what she assumed was the past several days. Cool cloths sponging her skin. A deep voice talking to her, filled with gentleness. Murmured prayers.

Surely… no. Surely it couldn't be.

She had to know. Tired though she was, she forced her eyes to open.

Immediately, her eyes traced the familiar strong line of his jaw, and the softness of his blue-green eyes, and the glow of his light brown hair in the firelight, and she knew it was Mike's hand wrapped around hers, and her heart skipped a beat.

His eyes were so gentle. "Hello." When he smiled, it felt like a sunbeam striking right into the center of her heart.

She stirred slightly. "Belle… and Wyatt," she whispered. Her voice felt cracked from disuse.

"They're just fine. They're with Emma," said Mike. He laughed softly. "Sounds like they're having a great time."

Selena relaxed against her pillows and closed her eyes for a moment. Mike's squeeze of her hand made her open them again.

"Drink some tea, Selena." His voice was so soft. "You need to get your strength back, but your fever's gone. You're going to be just fine."

With an effort, Selena sat up, and Mike propped her up with pillows. He held up the cup, and she managed to take it, trembling a little, and take a few deep, fortifying sips of the tea.

"Thank you," she whispered, handing it back.

"How do you feel?" he asked.

"Better." She relaxed against her pillows. "Tired, but better."

"That's good." Mike took her hand again. "That's very good."

She wanted to just lie here and enjoy staring at him, but she needed to know. "Have you…" She coughed. "Have you been here this entire time?"

His smile flickered. "Ma helped."

"But you were the one here with me most of the time," said Selena. "I remember it."

He looked away.

"Why would you do that?" Selena whispered. She coughed again. "Why would you be by my side all this time?"

Mike looked up at her again, and there was vulnerability in his blue-green eyes. He stroked her hand with his thumb and bit his lip before speaking.

"Ever since Clara died," he murmured, "I'd built a wall around my heart, protecting myself. I never wanted to lose anyone again, Selena. I never wanted to love and lose again. It was more than I thought I could bear."

Selena let out a sigh. "I can understand that."

"But when you got sick…" Mike shook his head. "I realized that I can never not love. And I realized that you'd climbed my walls." His eyes searched hers. "I realized that all my walls had done was to widen the terrible void in my heart."

Selena's breath caught. She said nothing, only gazed into his eyes, her heart thumping in her chest, and not from fever.

"That was a void that only you could fill." Mike smiled. "You and Wyatt and Belle."

Selena's heart skipped a beat.

"Spending time with you and the children made me realize that I do want a family, just as much as I always wanted one with Clara. And even though Clara is safely in her heavenly home now… I still want that family. I want *your* family," he whispered.

Selena didn't realize she was crying until the hot tear ran down her cheek.

"The truth is." Mike took a long breath. "I've fallen in love with you. And nothing in the world would make me happier than being your husband and a father to Wyatt and Belle."

"Oh, Mike," Selena whispered. "Oh, Mike, I'm in love with you too."

He laughed, a small and choked sound, but nonetheless joyous for it. "Then tell me, Selena, will you marry me?"

She couldn't stop smiling and crying and coughing all at once. It was messy and not particularly beautiful, but it was a moment she would never forget.

"Yes," she cried. "Yes."

And that was how the rest of her life began.

EPILOGUE

Two Years Later

The clattering of hooves on the road outside the general store caught Selena's attention. She looked up from behind the counter and through the main display window, gazing over the row of people waiting to be served. A whirlwind of boys and ponies thundered past in a cloud of dust, and Selena grimaced a little.

"Don't you fret." The miner waiting in front of her let out a chuckle. "It's the best way to grow up."

"Oh, I know it." Selena laughed as she handed him his supplies. "It just gives me gray hairs, that's all."

"It's all right, Mama," a small voice piped up behind her. "You don't have that many gray hairs."

Selena and most of the store burst out laughing. She turned to Belle, who was playing contentedly with her dolls on a blanket behind the counter. The four-year-old's angelic eyes were set in a round, rosy face filled with happiness. "Thank you, Belle, that was nice of you to say."

Belle giggled and hugged her cousin, two-year-old Benjamin. He squealed and pushed her away, but that had never stopped her from loving him.

A few moments later, the front door crashed open, and three boys strode into the store, covered in dust, thirsty, and clamoring for milk and candy. Wyatt was at their head. His blue eyes were brighter than ever, and he gave Selena a gap-toothed grin as she handed out gum balls.

"Hey, Ma," he said, his accent already holding a Colorado drawl. "Can we go riding down by the creek? I talked to Pa, and he said it was fine with him if it was fine with you."

Pa. Even after all this time, the sound of that name on his lips made her heart sing. "Sure, honey," she said. "Just don't go past the ridge."

"C'mon, boys," Wyatt burst out, and they all scattered.

Mike came in from the storeroom as Selena was busy serving the next customer. "Was that Wyatt?" he asked.

"Yes. He's going to play by the creek with his friends. I said it was all right," said Selena.

"He'll be just fine." Mike wrapped an arm around her shoulders and kissed her cheek. "He's a good boy."

"That he is," Selena smiled snuggling against him. "That he is."

The End

CONTINUE READING...

Thank you for reading *A Stranger's Children!* Are you wondering **what to read next?** Why not read *The Deserted Groom?* **Here's a peek for you:**

The first light dusting of snow was beginning to accumulate on the steps outside as the bride came down the aisle, a small bouquet of the last few black-eyed Susans in her hands. She was dressed in her mother's wedding gown, a gesture that was not to be overlooked in the small town of Culver's Creek, Missouri, steeped in tradition as it was. The veil was new, though; ordered special through the mercantile. In the marriage of his youngest daughter, the last to leave the house, Martin Connor was prepared to spare no expense.

The last of the daughters to leave the house, at least. The oldest of the four Connor siblings, and the only boy, stood with his mother in the second aisle, watching his youngest sister proceed past the gamut of admiring gazes. Martin let his eyes rest on the young man, feeling the familiar tug at his heart. His only son, the man who would inherit the ranch and carry on the family name. Martin loved all his children, but Val had a special spot in his heart. He could only hope that it wasn't as obvious to all as he feared it was.

He sighed, turning his gaze back to Lydia. She was just eighteen, and every inch the sweetest, prettiest bride Culver's Creek had ever seen – at least, since her two sisters got married. Yes, he was proud of all his children. If they could all see the same sort of happiness that was on Lydia's beaming face right this moment, he would go to his grave content.

His wife tucked her arm through his, stepping closer. She gave him a teary-eyed smile, her face filled with fondness and love, and he put a hand over hers, pressing warmly. His heart swelled with the happiness of the occasion – and, faintly, his fear for the future. He tried his best to push the thought away. There was no use borrowing trouble…

Martin resisted the urge to press a kiss to his wife's temple. It wasn't that the townsfolk in Culver's Creek would frown on such a public display of affection between an old married man and his wife, exactly – but he had something of a reputation to uphold in this town, even now.

He did allow himself to lean closer and whisper into her ear.

"You're as pretty as the day I married you, Bernice."

Visit HERE To Read More!
https://ticahousepublishing.com/mail-order-brides.html

THANKS FOR READING!

If you **love Mail Order Bride Romance, <u>Visit Here</u>**

https://wesrom.subscribemenow.com/

to find out about all <u>**New Susannah Calloway Romance Releases!**</u> **We will let you know as soon as they become available!**

If you enjoyed *A Stranger's Children*, would you kindly take a couple minutes to leave a positive review on Amazon? It only takes a moment, and positive reviews truly make a difference. Thank you so much! I appreciate it!

Turn the page to discover more Mail Order Bride Romances just for you!

MORE MAIL ORDER BRIDE
ROMANCES FOR YOU!

ABOUT THE AUTHOR

Susannah has always been intrigued with the Western movement - prairie days, mail-order brides, the gold rush, frontier life! As a writer, she's excited to combine her love of story with her love of all that is Western. Presently, Susannah lives in Wyoming with her hubby and their three amazing children.

www.ticahousepublishing.com
contact@ticahousepublishing.com